Impatient Pamela
Learns About
GERMS

Sarah Overland

Illustrated by Aaron Conway

Dedicated to three wonderful kids: Elias, Stella, and Maia,
who bring home every germ in town.

- Sarah Overland

Dedicated to my family.

- Aaron Conway

Trellis Publishing, Inc.
P.O. Box 16141
Duluth, MN 55816
800-513-0115

Impatient Pamela Learns About Germs

Publisher's Cataloging-in-Publication
(Provided by Quality Books, Inc.)

Overland, Sarah.
      Impatient Pamela learns about germs / Sarah Overland;
     illustrated by Aaron Conway.
     p. cm.
     SUMMARY: Impatient Pamela is a young girl afraid of germs and the illnesses they cause.
          She learns how washing her hands and other healthy habits can help protect
          her from getting sick. Her new understanding frees her to travel around the
          world, including visiting her pen pal, without fearing germs.
     Audience: Ages 4-8
     LCCN 2006920809
     ISBN-13: 978-1-930650-11-4 (Library hardcover ed.)
     ISBN-10: 1-930650-11-6
     ISBN-13: 978-1-930650-25-1 (Softcover ed.)
     ISBN-10: 1-930650-25-6

       1. Bacteria–Juvenile fiction. 2. Viruses–Juvenile
fiction. 3. Children–Health and hygiene–Juvenile
fiction. [1. Bacteria–Fiction. 2. Viruses–Fiction.
3. Cleanliness–Fiction.]   I. Conway, Aaron, ill.
II. Title.

PZ7.O949Imp 2006   [E]
                     QBI06-600029

10 9 8 7 6 5 4 3 2 1

Printed in China

Foreword

Dear Reader,

These days our children are exposed to many scary things. Violence, illness and injury seem to lurk around every corner – in the media, video games and sometimes in our own backyards. It is no wonder that even the youngest of children have some very adult worries! As parents we can not control everything our children are confronted with, but we can provide them with the knowledge and skills they need to help them have better, happier and healthier lives.

Being sick is a terrible feeling, whether you are age 5 or 85. Almost everyone dreads the thought of "catching" a cold, flu or other illness, yet few of us follow the basic rules that could easily prevent those problems. Washing our hands, covering our mouth while coughing, and keeping our fingers out of our mouth, nose and eyes all help stop the spread of germs. Our bodies give us most of the protection we need – we just have to support them along the way!

No matter how hard we try we can not stop the bad things from happening – but we can do our best. What better gift to give our children than the lifelong gift of better health? Thank you, Pamela, for showing children and reminding adults how easily they can make their world safer and less scary, and for giving us all one less thing to worry about.

Dr. Danielle C. Landis

Dr. Danielle C. Landis, Deputy Director of the Center for Leadership in Public Health Practice at the University of Southern Florida, College of Public Health, develops and coordinates state, national and international public health training programs. She works with public health and medical professionals around the world, including projects in the United States, the Caribbean, Central Asia, the former Soviet Republic, India, and South America. Her areas of expertise include leadership and crisis leadership development, international workforce development programs, and HIV/AIDS program planning.

Her Doctorate in Philosophy in Public Health from the University of South Florida included a concentration in social and behavioral science and a specialization in father/daughter communication and body image disturbances. Her master of public health specialization was in health education and social marketing.

One beautiful spring morning, Pamela woke up feeling terrible.

"You have a fever, Pamela. You'll have to stay home from school today," her mother said.

"But Mommmmm, I have a softball game this afternoon," Pamela whined.

"Sorry, Pamela, but you've caught a bad cold and it may take a few days for you to feel better."

"What do you mean I caught a cold? I wasn't trying to catch anything!" Pamela imagined holding out her softball mitt.

"Some germs got into your body and made you sick."

"What are germs?" Pamela asked.

"Germs are creatures so tiny that you can't see them."

"Like tiny bugs?"

"No, not exactly like bugs, but so small you can't even see them! Remember when you were at Martin's house the other day and he got sick? Did he sneeze and cough?"

"Yes," Pamela said, "he sneezed all over the place!!"

"When a sick person coughs or sneezes, germs spray into the air. When another person breathes in that air, they can get sick too. That's why you should cover your mouth when you sneeze or cough."

"When Dad got the flu, he didn't cough, and you got sick too, Momma."

"Germs pass from one person to another when we touch the same things. Right now this thermometer has your cold germs on it."

"So don't put it in your mouth, Momma," Pamela warned.

"I won't, but even if I touch the thermometer and then touch my face I could get sick. Germs can't get through your skin though. It's too tough for them."

"They need an opening, like the ones on your face."

"My mouth?" Pamela opened wide.

"Yes, and your nose and your eyes."

"Wow, germs are clever little creatures, Momma."

"They are, but if you wash your hands after you go to the bathroom and before you eat, you'll usually be okay."

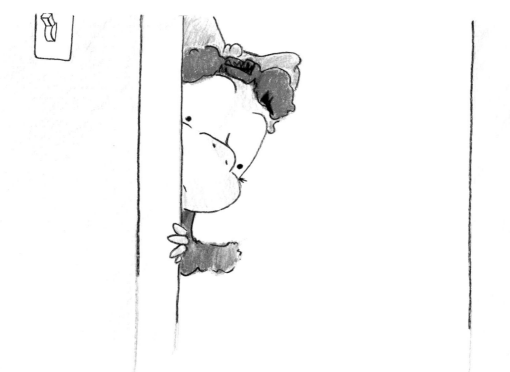

All day Pamela looked for germs everywhere…

…in her bedroom…

…near
Meow-Man…

…on her teddy bear…

…everywhere.

The next morning Pamela felt better. At breakfast, she decided not to touch anything. She didn't want to get sick again.

"Pamela, here's a letter from Kim, your pen pal," Pamela's father said.

"That's great!" said Pamela.

Kim lived far away. She and Pamela had never met, but they wrote to each other all the time. As she reached for the letter, she remembered about not touching anything.

"Could you read it to me, Dad?" Pamela asked.

Dear Pamela,

How are you? How is Meow-Man? I am in the hospital because my stomach really hurt. I had an operation to take out my appendix. I'm okay now and my Grandma is taking me for a treat tonight. I'm glad because the hospital smells bad, but I get to read books all day!

Your pen pal,
Kim

"DROP THE LETTER, DAD!! Kim touched that – you'll end up in the hospital!" Pamela shouted.

"Goodness, Pamela. I can't get sick from touching this letter. She had an infection you can't catch. There are lots of illnesses like that. Speaking of Kim, did you know that your Aunt Sally is going to a conference where Kim lives? You and your mom could go with her and visit Kim. What do you think about that?"

"Really? Would we get to ride in an airplane?"

"Yes," Pamela's dad nodded.

"Yippee, I want to go!" Pamela said. She thought about all the fun things she and Kim could do together.

Pamela had never flown in an airplane before. She could hardly wait.

"Can we go NOWWW, Momma?" Pamela asked impatiently every day. And every day Pamela's mother would just say, "Soon, Pamela. Very soon."

Pamela dreamt about airplanes and luggage and seeing her friend Kim.

Finally, it was the night before they were leaving. Her parents watched the news on TV. There were some people at the hospital, looking scared and wearing white masks like doctors use. Pamela knew they were trying not to breathe in germs.

"What's that?" asked Pamela. "Do those people have horrible germs?"

"No, honey, those people are being extra careful because there is a scary but very rare sickness in parts of the world."

Pamela went straight to her room.

"What do you think, Meow-Man?
Will this help? I'm going to pack this
in my carry-on and I will be ready for
anything."

At the airport the next day, Pamela took out her towel and wrapped it around her face.

Aunt Sally asked, "What are you doing, Pamela?"

"There might be germs here, and I don't want to get sick. You're a doctor, Aunt Sally. You should know to be more careful!"

"You don't have to worry about germs," Aunt Sally said. "Just remember to wash your hands, and keep your fingers out of your eyes, nose, and mouth. In the hospital I'm around sick people all the time, and I hardly ever get sick."

"You can take your towel off now."

"Okay, I'll put it back in my carry-on, but I'll keep it by me, just in case. Momma, are you sure we'll get our suitcases back? I've got my favorite soccer shoes in my bag, and the baseball cap I brought for Kim."

The man behind the ticket counter promised Pamela she'd get her suitcase as soon as the plane landed.

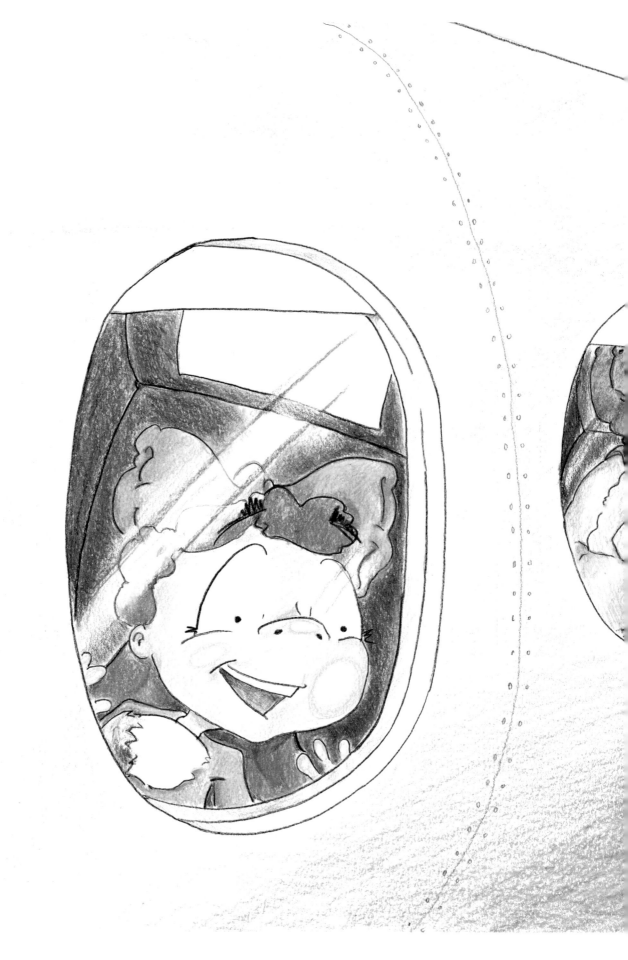

The flight attendant showed Pamela how to be safe on the airplane and helped her buckle her seat belt.

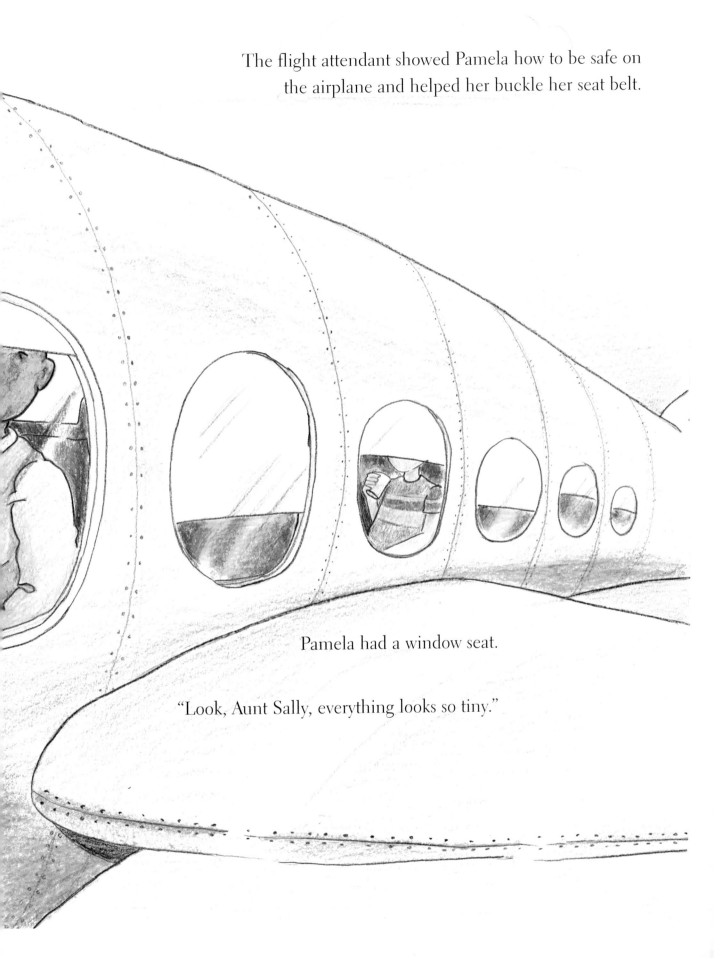

Pamela had a window seat.

"Look, Aunt Sally, everything looks so tiny."

The plane ride was long, but the flight attendants brought Pamela peanuts and juice and airplane stickers. She read her favorite book and then she took a nap.

Pamela woke up when the lady behind her started coughing. Pamela hoped the woman was covering her mouth. She reached for her towel.

"Are you okay, ma'am?" Pamela asked, wrapping her towel around her face.

"Yes, dear – it's just a frog in my throat."

"A FROG? I thought they were tiny creatures!
Aunt Sally, can I catch frogs?
I better go to the bathroom and wash
my hands."

"No, Pamela, that's just a saying that means her throat itches. She's not sick. You don't need to be afraid of germs. There are all kinds of tiny creatures in this world – germs, viruses, and bacteria. Your body has some kinds of bacteria in it that are good for you."

"You mean like how bats look kind of gross but they help us by eating lots of mosquitoes?" Pamela asked, folding up her towel. She thought of how once a bat had swooped over her head and scared her.

"Yes, just like that. Some bacteria help keep the world clean."

Pamela frowned. Aunt Sally was smart but who ever heard of
tiny creatures that were good?

"Your body can fight off lots of bad germs,
just like when you got better from your
cold, all by yourself."

"Am I fighting monsters and bugs?
Like in a video game?" Pamela asked.

"There are cells in your blood that eat up
the bad germs. And they are all different
shapes. Under a microscope, some look like
donuts, and some like earthworms. Some even
look like puffy clouds!!"

"Cool," said Pamela, feeling stronger.

"Your body is amazing. Most of the time it can heal itself. Have you ever had a scratch?"

"Sure I have," Pamela said, remembering when she went raspberry picking and got all scratched up from the branches.

"Your body healed itself, didn't it? When you checked under your bandage after a few days, it was all better, right?"

"Yeah, and I like the bandages with the cats on them. They work the best!"

"Sometimes your body needs a little help, and then you go to the doctor."

"Like when Martin broke his arm?"

"Right!"

"Or when Kim had to get her appendix out?"

"Exactly."

Pamela felt better, and just then the plane started to land.

At the baggage terminal, Pamela watched as suitcases rolled by.
Black ones, brown ones, bag after bag. Finally she
saw hers.

"There's my suitcase, Momma.
Grab it, grab it!"

Pamela could hardly wait to go out and
meet Kim. She had seen her picture.

"Do you think we'll recognize Kim, Momma?"

"I'm sure we will, Pamela."

Pamela looked all around, and
there was Kim, standing next to
her grandmother …

...waiting for Pamela.

Pamela forgot all about germs and her towel and ran to Kim.
She gave her a big hug, not one bit afraid of germs.
Kim wasn't afraid either, because she hugged her right back.